ABC *of* CHRISTIANITY *for kids*

ABC *of* CHRISTIANITY *for kids*

Barry O'Brien

ILLUSTRATIONS BY
Pearl D'Souza

ALEPH

ALEPH BOOK COMPANY
An independent publishing firm
promoted by ***Rupa Publications India***

First published in India in 2026 by
Aleph Book Company
161-B/4, Gulmohar House,
Yusuf Sarai Community Centre,
New Delhi 110049

ISBN: 978-93-6523-792-4

1 3 5 7 9 10 8 6 4 2

Design by Antra K
Printed in India

For Mrs Sweeney, my first catechism teacher at St Xavier's, for introducing me to the teachings of Christ.
For Fr Remedious, Fr Bouche, and Fr Van, for introducing me, through their lives, to the Ways of Christ.

INTRODUCTION

FOUR FACTS You Should Know Before You Read This Book

#1 Those who follow the teachings of Lord Jesus Christ are called Christians.

#2 The religion they follow is called Christianity. They are by faith Christians.

#3 To become a Christian, a person has to be baptized.

#4 Baptism is the name of the ceremony that welcomes a person to Christianity.

FIVE IMPORTANT PILLARS of Christianity

#1 BE LIKE JESUS
Get to know about Jesus Christ, his life and teachings.
Try to live like him.

#2 LOVE
Love God.
Remember that God loves you.
Love one another like God loves you.

#3 FORGIVE
Ask God to forgive you when you do something wrong.
God will forgive you.
You too should forgive those who hurt you.

‡4 PRAY

Make the time to talk to God. That is prayer.
Go to church on Sundays to worship God. Pray with others.
Also, pray at home, as a family.

‡5 HELP PEOPLE

Be generous.
Do not be selfish. Give others what they need.
Feed the hungry.
Visit the sick and the lonely.
Be honest. Speak the truth.
Be kind, patient, and humble.

FIVE THINGS to Remember

‡1 There are many different groups of Christians. The three biggest groups are Roman Catholics, Protestants, and Orthodox.

‡2 About half of the total population of Christians are Catholics. As of 2024, there are about 1.4 billion Catholics around the world.

‡3 People who belong to the Church of England are called Anglicans. They are Protestants.

‡4 All groups believe that God sent Jesus Christ, his only son, to save us. Christ died for our sake. He rose from the dead on the third day.

‡5 All Christians believe in the Holy Trinity–God, the Father; God, the Son; and God, the Holy Spirit.

A CHURCH AND 'THE CHURCH'

When you hear the word 'church' you immediately think of a building. Like Hindus pray in temples, Muslims pray in mosques, and Sikhs in gurdwaras, Christians go to worship God in churches.

That is true. The holy building where Christians go to worship is called a church.

But it doesn't only mean that. It also has a deeper meaning. When we speak about 'the Church', we are speaking about all the people who follow Jesus. They come together, to pray, sing, read from the Bible, and worship. They learn more about Jesus. They share Jesus's message of love with other people. They are united in Christ. Together, they are 'the Church'.

† A cathedral is a big church. It is the main church in a city.

† St Peter's Basilica is in Vatican City. It is the most important church for Catholics. Vatican City is a very small country near Rome in Italy.

† St Paul's Cathedral is in London. It is the most important church for Anglicans.

† There are many Christian saints. People who are very holy, and close to God, may become saints after they die.

† Christians usually name their churches, schools, colleges, and hospitals after saints.

† The short form for 'Saint' is 'St'.

Adam and Eve

On the first day, God said, 'Let there be light and darkness, day and night.' He then made the heaven (or sky) and earth. On the earth he created the seas, plants, fruits, and trees. This was followed by the creation of the stars, the sun, and the moon. After that He created the creatures that swim and the birds that fly, followed by the animals in the forest. Finally, God made humans. He named the first man Adam, and the first woman, Eve.

He did all of this in six days. On the seventh day, he rested.

He made Adam and Eve 'in his own image'. This means that God gave them special abilities. He made them more intelligent than all living creatures. He told them that everything on earth was theirs. He wanted them to live happily and 'multiply'; have a family of their own. After that, there would be many more families.

Surrounded by beautiful flowers, trees, animals, and birds, Adam and Eve began to live a beautiful life. The only thing God told them not to do was eat the apples from one of the trees in their home, the Garden of Eden.

One day, a serpent wanted Adam and Eve to do something bad. He tempted them to eat an apple from the Forbidden Tree. He told them that they would become as wise as God if they ate the fruits of that tree. Eve plucked the apple off the tree and took a bite. She then got Adam to eat the apple too.

This made God very sad and angry. Adam and Eve were also unhappy because they had disobeyed their Maker. God punished them by asking them to leave Paradise, the Garden of Eden. They would now have to lead a hard life, full of struggles.

A Message

We should not do anything that goes against God's will. We should not be tempted into doing something bad. We should not make the mistake that Adam and Eve made. That is a sin.

Bible

Most religions have a holy book. For Christians, it is the Holy Bible.

All Christians have a copy of the Bible at home. They read it from time to time. Some read a part of it every day. Each part has a different name.

After reading a section of the Bible, the reader says: 'The Word of God.'

‡ The Holy Bible is the bestselling book of all time. It has sold over 5 billion copies and has been translated into about 700 different languages.

‡ A person who is written about in the Bible is called a Biblical character.

Christ Is Crucified

Jesus healed the sick. He forgave those who had done wrong. He asked people to love one another. More and more people became his followers. This made many religious leaders angry. They wanted to crucify him.

They knew one of Jesus's friends. His name was Judas. He did not like everything that Jesus was doing. So, he agreed to tell the priests where they could find Jesus. They paid him thirty pieces of silver to do this. In other words, Judas betrayed his friend Jesus for thirty pieces of silver!

One evening, after having supper with Judas and his eleven other closest friends, Jesus went to the Garden of Gethsemane to pray. He knew he had to suffer to save people from their sins, so he asked his Father in Heaven to prepare him. He prayed to God to give him strength to bear the pain and suffering.

His friends, who were praying with him, were tired and soon fell asleep. That was when a group of soldiers surrounded Jesus. Judas had led them there to arrest him.

Peter, one of Jesus's friends, used a sword to cut off the right ear of Malchus, the servant of the high priest. But Jesus stopped Peter, saying, 'Put away the sword. All who take the sword shall die by the sword.' Jesus's other friends ran away in fear.

The guards took Jesus to Pontius Pilate, the governor of the Roman province of Judaea. After asking Jesus a few questions, Pilate told the religious leaders that he found nothing wrong with Jesus. But they kept telling Pilate that Jesus should be crucified. In the streets, crowds of people started shouting, 'Crucify him! Crucify him!'

Finally, the governor gave in to the peoples' demand, and Jesus was taken away by the soldiers. They tore off his clothes, whipped him, spat on him, and placed a crown of thorns on his head. They gave him a heavy wooden cross to carry. Though exhausted and bleeding, he was forced to drag the cross all the way up to the top of Mount Calvary. There, they nailed Jesus's hands and feet to the cross and raised it to stand in the centre, between the crosses of two petty thieves.

Being the Son of God, Jesus could have saved himself. But he knew he had to die to save people from their sins. So, he suffered on the cross and prayed for those who were killing him. A little later, he died, with these words on his lips, 'Father, into your hands I commit my spirit. It is finished.'

Two friends of Jesus, Joseph of Arimathea and Nicodemus, placed his body in a tomb and rolled a heavy stone in front of it.

Two thousand years later, Christians thank Jesus Christ and bow before him for dying on the cross to save them. They perform this action on Good Friday, the day on which he gave up his life for his people.

‡ In ancient times, in places like Rome and Persia, people were crucified. To be crucified meant being punished and put to death by being nailed to a cross.

‡ You will often see crucifixes in churches and Christian homes. A crucifix is a cross with an image of Jesus on it.

Disciples and Apostles

At the age of thirty, Jesus left home. He travelled from one place to another, telling people that God wanted them to love one another. Many people liked what he said and learned a lot from him. They became his disciples or friends. Among them, there were twelve who never left his side. They were his Apostles–his very special friends.

They were not teachers, businessmen, or priests. Jesus chose twelve simple men. Andrew and his brother Peter, and James and his brother John were fishermen. It is most likely that Thomas, Thaddeus, Bartholomew, and Philip were also fishermen. Matthew was a tax collector. The others in this special group were James, the son of Alpheus, and Simon Zelotes. Judas was incharge of the group's money. After betraying Jesus, he felt guilty and hanged himself. He was later replaced by Matthias.

The Bible tells us that, right up to Jesus's death, his Apostles were anything but brave. They were easily frightened. When they saw the soldiers arresting Jesus, most of them ran away in fear. Later, early in the morning, before the cock crowed twice, Peter was asked whether he was a friend of Jesus. He denied it three times, saying 'No, I have never met the man.' He was afraid that he too would be killed.

Then, after Jesus was crucified, they were so afraid that they hid in a room. Suddenly, Jesus appeared in the middle of the room, though it was locked from the inside. They were confused and terrified. He greeted them and showed them the wounds on his hands and his side. It was then that they realized that their teacher had risen from the dead.

Jesus then spent all his time preaching to them. He taught them many things and filled their hearts with courage. After forty days, he went to the Mount of Olives, where he told them to spread his message of love and his teachings. He then ascended into heaven. This is called the Ascension.

After this, the Apostles changed completely. The same men who had been cowards for so long were now brave and fearless. They travelled to many places preaching the Gospel. While doing this, almost all of them were killed. They became martyrs.

Preaching the Gospel means spreading God's message of love and sharing the good news about Jesus Christ–that he died, was buried, and he rose again.

Easter

You have read about how Jesus was crucified on what is now known as Good Friday. The day before that is the day on which Jesus had his Last Supper with his twelve Apostles. It is called Maundy Thursday.

On the third day after his death, Mary Magdalene and some other women who were Jesus's followers, went to the tomb. They noticed that the stone had been rolled away and the tomb was empty. Since they did not know where Jesus's body was, they were scared and confused. A little later, Mary Magdalene saw a man whom she thought was the gardener. She soon realized that the man was Jesus. He had risen from the dead. She ran straight to the Apostles to give them the Good News.

The people who crucified Jesus thought that by killing him they would put an end to him and his teachings. Christians believe that that God loves his people too much to let sin defeat them and keep them away from him. That is why he sent Jesus, his Son, to save them. And that is the Good News that is celebrated on Easter Sunday–the Resurrection of Christ.

A long service is held at every church where people pray, sing, and read parts of the Bible. This is how they celebrate the joy of welcoming the Risen Christ. After that, people come together to spread the joy of Easter.

On the fun side, children look forward to getting Easter eggs, while adults enjoy some hot cross buns!

Forgive

Even while he was dying on the cross, Jesus forgave the people who were killing him. He prayed to God, 'Father, forgive them, for they do not know what they are doing.'

Christians are taught to forgive even those who hurt them. It is not easy, but that is what they are expected to do.

The Bible says not to take 'an eye for an eye, and a tooth for a tooth.' If we harm someone who has harmed us, people would be violent or mean all the time. Mahatma Gandhi said something very similar: 'An eye for an eye will make the whole world blind.'

What about people who commit sins? Does God forgive them? Most certainly! That is why Christians say this to God: 'Forgive us our sins, as we forgive those who sin against us.'

Christians are also encouraged to go to confession as often as they can or need to. They confess their sins to God, they tell a priest about the wrong things they have done. The priest cannot see who they are. He blesses them and tells them that God has forgiven them. They should try not to sin again.

Gospel

A very important part of the Holy Bible is called the Gospel or 'the good news'. It tells us the story of Jesus's birth, death, and resurrection.

There are four Gospels. They were written by different saints–Matthew, Mark, Luke, and John. They are called the Evangelists.

There are many evangelists now. An evangelist is a person who shares Jesus's message with others. This message is about love and forgiveness, and about being kind to people and helping them.

At every Holy Mass or prayer service in church, a passage from one of the Gospels is read. The priest tells the congregation which Gospel that reading has been taken from. A congregation is a group of people who come together to worship and pray to God.

Holy Trinity

The Holy Trinity is a way of describing God the Father, God the Son, and God the Holy Spirit. Christians believe that there is one God. They also believe that there are three persons in one God–the Father, the Son, and the Holy Spirit.

Many years ago, I told my catechism teacher, Mrs Sweeney, that I could not understand this. Since I was a child, she tried to explain it in a simple way. She said to me, 'An egg has a yolk, an albumen, and a shell. All three parts make the egg whole. There will be no egg if one of the parts are not there.'

‡ Christians make the Sign of the Cross before and after they pray.

‡ While making the Sign of the Cross, Christians say, 'In the name of the Father, and of the Son, and of the Holy Spirit, Amen.'

1
2
3
4

INRI

The next time you see a crucifix or a painting of the Crucifixion, look carefully at it. You will see INRI written on the cross just above Jesus's head. It stands for the Latin words 'Iesus Nazarenus, Rex Iudaeorum'. Now, don't try to read that! Just remember that it means, 'Jesus of Nazareth, the King of the Jews'. The Roman emperor Pontius Pilate had it written on the cross.

The chief priests of the Jews told Pilate that Jesus said he was the King of the Jews though he was not their king. Pilate told them to let it be and not change what had already been written.

Why was it written in Latin?

Because it was the official language of the Roman empire.

Joseph and Mary

A little over 2,000 years ago, there lived a man named Joseph. He was a simple, hardworking carpenter and was soon to be married to a young girl named Mary.

One day, God sent an angel to Mary. The angel's name was Gabriel. He said to her, 'Do not be afraid. I have come to tell you that God will be sending his special Son. God loves you and has chosen you to give birth to him.'

An angel also told Joseph about this in a dream: 'Mary's son will be named Jesus. It means "Saviour" because he will save his people.'

Soon after, Joseph and Mary were married.

Nazareth (a town in Galilee, now part of Israel), the place where Joseph and Mary lived, was part of the Roman Empire. The emperor Augustus wanted to count how many people there were in his empire to make sure they paid their taxes. He ordered everyone to return to the town where their families belonged to and register their names.

Because of this, Joseph and his pregnant wife, Mary, had to travel all the way from Nazareth to Bethlehem, Joseph's birthplace. When they arrived in Bethlehem, they were very tired. They went from one inn to another, but on every door that they knocked they were told, 'There's no room at the inn!'

Finally, they were told by an innkeeper that they could rest for the night with his sheep, donkeys, and cows in a stable. So, that's what they did!

Later, on this special silent night, Mary gave birth to baby Jesus. Christians celebrate the birth of the Saviour every year on Christmas Day.

Kingdom of God

Every king or queen has a kingdom. It is the country or place he or she rules over.

Jesus is Christ the King–the King of Kings. When Pontius Pilate was questioning him, Jesus replied, 'My kingdom is not of this world.' What did Jesus mean by this?

The Kingdom of God means where God is in charge. It is where he takes care of people and things. That is his Kingdom. This means that when people are good to others, the Kingdom of God is in their hearts.

When we help those in need, those who are sick, and those who are in trouble, we are entering the Kingdom of God.

By doing what God wants us to do, we can live in God's Kingdom, now and forever.

Love

Jesus said, 'Love one another just as I have loved you.' It is every Christian's duty to spread His message of love.

Jesus explained that it was easy to love people who love you, like your parents and friends. But we should also try and love those who do not like us. We should not be mean to them if they are mean to us. Instead, we should pray for them.

Here are a few more messages from the Holy Bible about love:

‡ Whoever does not love does not know God, because God is love.

‡ Be humble, gentle, and patient with people. Show them that you love them.

‡ If you hate someone, it will lead to quarrels, but love makes up for all offences.

Christians are always reminded that it is not enough to read and speak about love. They must show their love through their actions, just as Jesus did. They can do this by helping the poor, the sick, children, and those who are elderly and cannot take care of themselves.

Miracles

Jesus performed many miracles. He did this to help people. It showed that he was the Son of God. He healed the sick. He made the blind see, the deaf hear, and the lame walk.

His first miracle happened at a wedding feast in Cana. When there was no more wine to serve the guests, he changed water into wine.

When Jesus and his disciples were on a boat out at sea, a terrible storm arose. The sea was so rough they were sure that they were about to die. Jesus calmed the sea and the storm with a command.

One day, about 5,000 people were listening to him preach. After a while, they became hungry. But there was nothing to feed them except five loaves of bread and two small fishes. Jesus prayed and made the food multiply. Soon there was plenty of food, and there was even some left over after everyone had eaten.

Then there was the time when the disciples saw their Master walking on the water to reach them. They were on a boat far from the shore.

Noah, Moses, and Abraham

There are many good people you can read about in the Old Testament of the Bible.

One of them is Noah. When God was unhappy with his people, he decided to cause a flood. Noah was the only person God spoke to about this. God told him to build an ark–a large boat made of wood. This special boat would keep Noah, his family, and the animals and birds safe.

When people saw Noah building the ark, they thought he was mad. They said, 'It is not raining, and there is no river or sea here, yet he is building an ark!'

Later, when it rained for forty days and nights, everyone died except Noah's family, and the creatures that were in the ark.

You will also get to know about Abraham.

For Christians, he is the father of the faith–the father of all who believe in God. Our Muslim brothers and sisters are said to be the descendants of Ishmael, Abraham's son.

You will also meet Moses.

Pharoah announced that all Hebrew newborn babies would be killed. Moses's mother wanted to save him, so she placed the baby in a basket and set it afloat on the river. The basket floated down the Nile until one of Pharaoh's daughters found it. She took care of Moses in the palace as if he was her own son.

One day, God appeared to Moses in a burning bush. God told him to return to Egypt. With God's help, Moses freed the Israelites from their slavery.

ld and New Testaments

The Holy Bible is made of two parts: the Old Testament and the New Testament.

In the Old Testament, you will read about God's laws and the history of Israel before Jesus Christ was born.

The first part is called the Book of Genesis It tells us how God created the world, the early history of humanity, and the origins of the Jewish people.

The New Testament contains the story of Jesus. It explains how the world and all of us were saved because he died for our sins.

The New Testament was written between 50 and 100 years after the death of Christ. It was originally written in Greek by many different authors.

Parable

A parable is a simple story that teaches a lesson or gives a message. To help their students become better people, good teachers often speak to them in parables.

Jesus was a great teacher and a master storyteller. He shared many meaningful messages with his friends and followers through his parables. You can read these easy-to-understand stories in the Bible. This is one of my favourites.

THE PARABLE OF THE GOOD SAMARITAN

A Jewish man was lying on the side of a road. He had been robbed and severely beaten by bandits. First, a priest walked past him without helping him. After that, a Levite (a person who helped priests with their work) passed him. The injured man had expected these two Jewish men, who loved God, to help him. But neither of them did. Finally, a Samaritan came along. Jews and Samaritans hated each other, so the dying man was sure that this passerby would ignore him. But what happened was quite different!

The Samaritan did whatever he could to help the stranger– his Jewish brother. He treated his wounds, applied medicine and bandaged them, and lifted him onto his donkey. He took him to an inn, gave the innkeeper some money, and asked him to take good care of the injured man.

The message to us from this parable is: 'Love ALL people and show kindness to them–not only to those from your own family, community, or country.'

If someone helps another person in a kind and generous manner, we call that person, a good Samaritan. Now you know why!

Quiz

Since it not possible to include everything important about Christianity in this little book, here is a short quiz. The questions focus on people or events not mentioned in this book.

†1 The Egyptian soldiers of Pharaoh were chasing the Israelites. That's when Moses parted the Red Sea and saved his people. The land in the middle became dry, and the Israelites walked through. What happened to Pharaoh's army?

†2 He got his strength from his hair. When his long hair was cut off by Delilah, he lost his strength. Who was he?

†3 King Darius wanted people to pray to him. Because this man prayed to God, he was thrown into a den of lions by the king. But God protected the man, and the lions did not attack. What was his name?

†4 What did Jesus wash during the Last Supper on Maundy Thursday?

†5 Which of his Twelve Apostles did Jesus call the rock upon which he would 'build his Church'?

†6 A nun who started caring for the poor and sick in Kolkata was declared a saint by the Catholic Church after her death. Who was she?

ANSWERS

1. As soon as they followed the Israelites into the dry land, the water from the sea flowed back, and all the soldiers were drowned.
2. Samson.
3. Daniel.
4. The feet of his twelve Apostles.
5. Simon, better known as Peter—Peter means 'rock'. He went on to lead the Church as the first Pope.
6. Saint Teresa of Kolkata, also known as Mother Teresa, the founder of the Missionaries of Charity.

Religious and Laity

The word 'religious' is used to describe a person who follows a particular religion. He or she believes in God.

But it also has another meaning. We use the word 'religious' to refer to priests, nuns, and monks who take a vow to serve God. They are also called the clergy.

Come, let's meet some members of the clergy!

‡ **Parish Priests**: priests who look after the people in their area. They visit his parish or church.

‡ **Vicar or Reverend**: other words for priest.

‡ **Bishop, Archbishop, Cardinal**: very senior priests.

‡ **Pope**: the head of the Catholic Church.

‡ **The Archbishop of Canterbury**: the head of the Anglican Church.

Christians who are not priests or nuns are called the laity. So, the Church is made up of the clergy and the laity.

Seven Sacraments

A sacrament is a religious ceremony or ritual at which Christians receive divine grace. 'Receiving a divine grace' means being blessed by God in a special way.

The first two sacraments that Christians usually receive are Baptism and First Holy Communion (or Eucharist). The other five sacraments are Confirmation, Penance, Matrimony, Holy Orders, and the Anointing of the Sick.

‡ **Baptism**: Only when people are baptized do they become Christians. They make a promise to believe in God the Father, the Son, and Holy Spirit, and to live as good Christians. The priest pours a little holy water on their forehead and welcomes them into the Church.

‡ **First Communion/Eucharist**: For Christians, receiving the Body and Blood of Jesus Christ in the form of bread and wine, is called the Eucharist. After receiving this sacrament they are are able to partake in the Body and Blood of Christ.

‡ **confirmation**: For Catholics, this sacrament follows Baptism and First Communion. It takes place when a Christian understands the faith more deeply.

‡ **Penance/Reconciliation/confession**: This sacrament gives Catholics the opportunity to confess their sins and be sorry for them. God forgives them.

‡ **Holy Matrimony**: A ceremony at which two people take their marriage vows, promising to live together as husband and wife for the rest of their lives.

‡ **Holy orders/ordination**: Those who become priests and nuns or join the Holy Order to serve God take this sacrament. They make special promises to God of how they will serve him and help people.

‡ **Anointing of the sick**: A special blessing is given to a person who is very sick. It is usually given when a person is dying. The person is anointed with holy oil.

At a Holy Mass or service in church, water and wine are blessed by the priest. They represent the Body and Blood of Christ, which are then distributed to the Christians present at the service.

Ten Commandments

Whether we are on a street, a train or a bus, at school or at home, we have to follow rules. This helps us to become disciplined.

God loves us. That is why he gave us commandments or instructions to follow. They help us in being good and kind. They tell us how we can be safe and keep others safe too.

God spoke to Moses on Mount Sinai. He gave him the Ten Commandments, written on two stone tablets. Moses told the people to follow these commandments and lead a good life.

These are God's Ten Commandments:

#1 I am your Lord, you should not worship any other gods.

#2 You should not make idols and worship them.

#3 You should show respect to God and not say His name in a bad way.

‡4 Take a day of rest from work, and honour God on that day.

‡5 Love and respect your father and mother.

‡6 You should not commit murder.

‡7 Those who are married should keep the promises they make to their partner on their wedding day.

‡8 Do not steal.

‡9 Do not tell lies to save yourself or get other people into trouble. Speak the truth.

‡10 Be happy with what you have. Do not be greedy and desire what other people have.

Moses was a leader and prophet. A prophet is a wise and knowledgeable teacher. He guides people and tells them about what God wants them to do.

nworthy

'Unworthy' is a word used to describe people who do wrong things. They are not good enough to be respected by others.

But God never finds us to be unworthy. Even when we sin, God forgives us. He wants us to feel sorry about what we have done and try not to sin again. He wants us to repent.

One of the parables that Jesus told his disciples was about the Prodigal Son. (We use the word 'prodigal' to describe a person who is wasteful and spends money too easily.) It is about a rich man and his two sons. The younger one takes his share of the wealth and leaves home. He enjoys himself with his friends and spends all his money. After some time, he has no money left. He ends up working as a servant in someone's house. He realizes that he has made a terrible mistake. He repents for his sins and returns home. He asks his father to take him back as a servant. But his father forgives him and welcomes him back as a son.

The elder son gets very upset. He says to his father, 'You are having a party to welcome my brother back. I was with you all this time, but you did not have any party for me.'

The father tells his elder son how much he loves him and how happy he is that he did not sin. But he makes him understand that those who sin should be forgiven.

The Message

God too wants us to reconcile with him. (To reconcile is to become friends again with someone.)

He will always forgive us and make us feel loved once again. This is called reconciliation.

Virtues

The meaning of the word 'virtue' in the dictionary is 'behaviour or attitude that show high moral standards'. This means behaviour and actions which are good and not wrong.

St Paul lists the nine most important virtues for a person to have. They are love, joy, peace, patience, kindness, generosity, faithfulness, gentleness, and self-control.

There are many Christian saints. They were people of God who were special in some way. St Paul was one of them. Before he became a follower of God, he killed many of Christ's followers. After that, he transformed completely. He did his best to spread Christ's message of love and peace.

A very important part of the New Testament is the Acts of the Apostles. A large part of it tells us about St Paul's travels, preaching, and the miracles he performed.

Wisdom

A wise person is one who knows a lot and uses that knowledge to make good decisions. He is said to possess wisdom. Another word we could use to describe the person would be 'sensible'.

The Bible tells us about some people who were unwise and acted foolishly. But it also introduces us to many who applied their wisdom to help themselves and others. One of them was Solomon.

Solomon, the son of David, loved God. After his father died, he became the king of Israel. One night, God appeared to Solomon in a dream. He asked him what he wanted. Solomon told God that he wanted to know how to rule his kingdom well. He wanted to be good to his people. He wanted his people to live happily.

God gave him the gift of wisdom. Solomon went on to become a very wise and kind ruler. His people loved and respected him. He also became rich and popular.

Xmas

You already know that Mother Mary gave birth to Jesus Christ, the Son of God. As soon as he was born, she wrapped a long piece of cloth around him and kept him in a manger (a long open box in which food for farm animals is placed). This happened in Bethlehem, a little over 2,000 years ago.

Later that night, the angels said to the shepherds, who were looking after their sheep in the fields, 'Glory to God, and peace to His people on earth. Today a Saviour has been born to us. You will find him lying in a manger.'

After the shepherds went to Bethlehem, they found Mary and Joseph. They saw baby Jesus lying in a manger. They soon told everyone about this.

High up in the sky, a bright new star appeared. Three kings from different countries saw the star. They were very educated and wise. They knew that a bright new star would appear when a great king was born. So, they left their homes to find the new king. Since there were three of them, we call them 'The Three Wise Men'. Their names were Caspar, Melchoir, and Balthasar.

They carried with them gifts of gold, frankincense (incense), and myrrh (embalming oil). The Three Wise Men followed the star for many days. When they arrived, they bowed down and placed their gifts next to baby Jesus.

The birthday of Jesus is now celebrated as Christmas Day on 25 December by Christians and many other people around the world. The first thing they do on this very special day is go to church. They pray for peace in the world, and for people to follow Jesus's message to love one another. Some even go to church for midnight Mass on 24 December.

Christmas Day is a day of celebration and happiness. People decorate their homes, they place a Christmas tree inside the house. They wear nice clothes, eat good food and Christmas cake. During the Christmas season, many people help others in some way or the other. Some choir groups sing Christmas carols, people visit friends and family, and offer assistance to the elderly or the homeless. And, of course, Santa Claus spreads the joy of Christmas by giving children gifts and wishing them 'Merry Christmas', followed by, 'Ho...ho...ho!'

Why is 'Christmas' also known as 'Xmas'?

The name 'Christ' comes from the Greek word 'Christos', meaning 'anointed one'. The Greek letter 'chi' is written like we write an 'x'.

So, Christmas = Xmas.

Yahweh

For the Israelites, in ancient times, Yahweh was one of God's names.

In the Bible, God is known by other names. Some of them are Jehovah, Abba Father, Adonai, Alpha, and Omega.

These are different ways of calling The Almighty or the one who is all powerful. God is the Alpha and the Omega, the beginning and the end.

Zion

In the Bible, Zion is often used as a name for Jerusalem or the Land of Israel.

Zion is a holy city protected by God. His people live there and serve Him.